Trapped!

Titles in
the Storykeepers series

Trapped!

Brian Brown and Andrew Melrose

ZondervanPublishingHouse
Grand Rapids, Michigan

A Division of HarperCollinsPublishers

For Karen and Pamela, Amy and Emma,
Joshua and Jessica, Yasmine and Jonny

Trapped!
Copyright © 1997 by Brian Brown and Andrew Melrose

Requests for information should be addressed to:

Zondervan Publishing House
Grand Rapids, Michigan 49530

First published in the UK by Cassell plc, London.

ISBN 0-310-20352-X

97 98 99 00 01 02 /* XX/ 10 9 8 7 6 5 4 3 2 1

Printed and bound in Great Britain
by The Guernsey Press Co. Ltd, Guernsey, Channel Isles

Contents

Chapter 1

Birthday Plans

"Okay, everybody," said Ben. "Be alert today. The streets are crawling with soldiers."

Anna was looking out a window of the bakery, watching as Roman soldiers ransacked shops just down the street. She saw them take wood from the carpenter and bolts of fabric from the seamstress. The soldiers didn't pay the shopkeepers. They just took whatever they wanted. Two soldiers even went into a fruit stand and took a basket of fruit without paying and started handing out the fruit to other soldiers, laughing as they did it.

Streets all over Rome were being decorated for Nero's birthday. Soldiers were already building frames with the wood they had taken and draping the fabric in wild banners. The poor shop owners could only stand and watch.

"I can't believe tomorrow is Nero's birthday again," said Anna, still watching from the window. "Why, his last one seems like only yesterday."

"That's because it was only three months ago," chipped in Justin. "Nero enjoyed himself so much he decided that since he is the emperor, he's entitled to more birthdays than the rest of us."

Anna nodded. Only ten, she was just as wise as thirteen-year-old Justin. Anna and Justin and Justin's four-year-old brother, Marcus, had been separated from their parents after the great fire of Rome, which destroyed much of the city. The children had been living on the streets of Rome until Ben found them and brought them home to live at the bakery with him and his wife, Helena.

"But why did the Empress Poppaea have to pick our bakery to cook for Nero's party?" asked eight-year-old Cyrus, an African juggler who also lived with Ben and Helena. He was rolling pieces of dough into special shapes and putting them in a baking pan.

"I'm sorry for all the trouble," said Miriam, who also was helping. She tugged nervously at the hem of her apron and kept her eyes down. "I suggested using the palace bakers, but the empress wouldn't listen. After all, I'm just one of her lowly servants."

"Don't apologize, Miriam," said Ben, his chubby face getting even redder as he pulled a pan of bread out of the oven.

Miriam smiled at Ben. Most people smiled at Ben. He

had that effect on just about everyone.

Ben slid the hot pan of bread onto the counter and wiped his hands on his apron. "There is nothing wrong with being a servant. It's an honorable occupation. Besides, we're just thankful there are Christians like you working in Nero's palace."

Comforted by his words, Miriam smiled again and sat down on a stool to watch the children as they helped Ben prepare the next batch of bread.

"Why do we knead the dough?" said Ben with a chuckle, looking down at the children and giving them a wink.

"Because everybody needs the bread," the children replied in unison.

Miriam laughed. This joke was a regular routine for Ben and the children, but this was the first time Miriam had heard it.

Just then, there was a loud pounding on the door.

Everyone froze.

"Open up in the name of Nero!" came the command.

The children scurried closer to Ben and looked toward the door with big, frightened eyes. They had all heard the same pounding, that same command when their parents were taken away.

"Shh!" Ben whispered to the children. "Keep quiet."

He turned to the door, his face suddenly serious.

Chapter 2

Miriam + Tacticus

"Open up!" came the deep voice again.

Ben walked over to the door of the bakery and turned the handle. As the door creaked open on its hinges, the tall, powerful figure of a Roman centurion filled the whole door frame and blocked out most of the light from the afternoon sun. His bronze helmet gleamed, and a large sword hung by his side.

"Tacticus!" shouted Anna suddenly.

The Roman centurion smiled, then walked into the bakery. "Hope I didn't scare you, but I had to make it sound official," he said, looking at Anna. Then he whispered something to Ben.

Ben hurried over to a cupboard and took out a breadboard. He turned it over. Hidden on the bottom was a disguised map of the city of Rome.

"Hmm," muttered Ben, tracing his finger over one area of the map. "You're right. The abandoned mill will be perfect for tonight's meeting. Good work, Tacticus."

But Tacticus wasn't listening to Ben. He was busy trying to catch Miriam's eye. When she did look up at him, he smiled at her. Startled, Miriam quickly looked down at the floor again.

"Tacticus?" said Ben.

"Uh, thanks, Ben," said the centurion, standing a bit straighter as he looked back at the map and pointed at one area of the city. "I reassigned the guards in that sector, so you shouldn't have any problems."

"But Tacticus," said Anna, "won't you be there?"

"I'm afraid not, Anna," replied the centurion, smiling at the girl.

He and Anna had had a special relationship ever since she had saved his life. Anna and Justin had been in the catacombs, Rome's underground cemetery, when there was a cave-in. Tacticus, who had been chasing them, had fallen down a shaft and would have died if Anna hadn't helped him, even though it meant she was putting herself in danger. Together she and Justin had pulled the Roman centurion to safety. He had been their friend from then on.

"I can't come tonight, Anna," Tacticus explained, "because Nero has demanded an audience with his closest advisers, and I must attend."

"Oh," Anna said softly. She was disappointed.

"Don't worry, Anna," said Helena, who had just entered the room. "We should be thankful that Nero is so fond of Tacticus." Then, turning to Tacticus, she said, "I'd hate to think what Nero would do if he found out you were a Christian."

The centurion smiled, remembering the day when he realized why Anna had saved his life. "Only my closest friends know that—and I plan to keep it that way."

"Well," added Ben, "you're not the first to keep such a secret. For a long time even Jesus' closest friends didn't know who he really was."

"They didn't know his name was Jesus?" asked Cyrus.

"Oh, they knew his name," Ben said, "but they didn't know he was God's chosen one, until …" Ben paused, then said, "Come, gather round, all of you. Nero's party pastries can wait. I have a story to tell you."

Ben sat down, but not before he had reached for one of his special pastries. He was a bit too fond of his own baking, and his waistline showed it.

Helena shook her head. "Ben," she chided with a smile, "you'll get even fatter."

"Helena," Ben said, an impish grin on his face, "one pastry can't do any harm. It's so small. Anyway, just listen, everyone.

"One day, Jesus led his disciples to the top of a mountain. It was a little misty that day, but as they reached the top, shafts of light pierced through the mist. At the summit Jesus, who had been walking a few steps ahead of his disciples, turned to face them. That's when an amazing thing happened."

"What happened?" asked Cyrus, anxiously.

"Yes, what?" Marcus echoed. Little Marcus had become very fond of Cyrus and often repeated what he said.

"Well," said Ben, smiling at the two youngsters, "Jesus' clothes began to sparkle, and glistened in a gleaming white light."

"Wow!" said Anna, her eyes big in amazement.

"You know, Anna," said Ben, "that's what the disciples might have said. They were certainly very surprised, perhaps even a little frightened."

"But why would they be frightened of Jesus?" asked Cyrus.

"Hush, Cyrus," urged Justin. "Let Ben finish."

Ben said, "As Jesus' clothes sparkled …"

"Ooh! I would like to have seen that," said Cyrus. "My father used to have a sparkly cloak. That was before …" Cyrus stopped, suddenly sad. "Before the great fire."

"I know," said Ben as he ruffled the youngster's hair.

Tacticus bent down and picked up Cyrus, who had been sitting on the floor, and settled the boy on his knee.

"As Jesus' clothes sparkled, two men appeared

alongside him," Ben said.

"Who were they?" asked Cyrus.

"One was a man of God called Elijah. Long before Jesus' time, he was a fierce fighter for God. The other," said Ben, "was another great hero. It was Moses, who led the Jewish people out of Egypt. Anyway, as Jesus stood with Elijah and Moses, the mist began to thicken. Then a voice was heard, saying:

"'This is my son. You must do what he says.'

"Then, just as suddenly as the mist had appeared, it vanished, and Jesus was standing alone, perfectly normal again. The disciples could hardly believe what they had seen.

"A little later, as they walked down from the mountain, Peter stopped for a moment and turned to look back at the summit. Jesus walked over to him and said, 'Do not tell anyone what you have seen until I am risen from the dead.'

"Peter nodded, but he did not understand, and neither did any of the other disciples. They didn't know what Jesus meant when he said 'risen from the dead.' You see," said Ben, as he looked straight at Tacticus, "Jesus knew it wasn't the right time to reveal who he really was."

"I can understand how he felt," replied the centurion as he rose to leave. "Thanks, Ben. I hope all goes well tonight." Tacticus shook Ben's hand. Then he ruffled Justin's hair affectionately.

Anna walked him to the door. "See you soon?" she asked.

Tacticus stopped at the door and rubbed a smudge of flour off Anna's nose. "I hope so." He smiled at Anna, then turned to Miriam, whom he recognized from the Imperial Palace. His face got a little red, then he said, a little shyly, "Uh, um, nice seeing you again, uh …"

Anna was surprised at the way Tacticus was acting. This wasn't like him at all. And when Miriam didn't answer right away, Anna gave Nero's servant a questioning look and said, "Miriam?"

Miriam smiled meekly at the tall Roman soldier. Looking up at him, she said, "It was good seeing you again too, Tacticus." She had noticed him at the palace too.

Tacticus gave a polite nod, then walked out of the bakery.

Anna, who had watched this little scene closely, got a twinkle in her eye and said, "Tacticus is really nice, isn't he, Miriam?"

Miriam sighed. "He certainly is." Then she noticed that Anna had scrawled "Miriam + Tacticus" in the flour on the baking counter.

"Anna!" giggled Miriam, quickly rubbing her fingers

through the flour to erase the words.

"All right, everybody," Ben said. "Better get back to work. The first delivery is due at the palace by nightfall, and our customer isn't exactly the patient type."

Anna rolled her eyes. "That's for sure!" she agreed.

Chapter 3

Caesar the Divine

Nero tapped his foot impatiently as dozens of workers struggled to haul in a massive marble bust.

"Hurry up, you lethargic lunks!" bellowed Nero, a scowl on his face. "Anyone who drops the new statue of me will go straight to the lions. And get that altar over here. How can I burn incense to myself if I have no altar?"

The workers gently set the bust of Nero on the floor. It was to be placed on top of the altar.

Then they pushed and shoved and grunted as they moved the heavy altar, inch by inch, across the floor.

"Why, Nero," said Nihilus, watching as they moved the altar, "your new altar is very impressive."

"Of course it is!" spluttered Nero. "Would I have an unimpressive altar, Nihilus?"

"Of course not," said Nihilus, a bit fearful of the

emperor's reaction. Even a Roman soldier as powerful as Nihilus wasn't safe around Nero.

"It's more than impressive," said Nero's chief toady, Snivilus, walking quickly toward the emperor. "It's stupendous! The most stupendous altar ever erected by a ruler to himself!"

"Ruler!" roared Nero. "I am no mere ruler, you sniveling little toad. I am a god!"

"That is what I meant!" said Snivilus, bowing before Nero. "You're the kind of god who rules over other gods. That's what I meant to say." He quickly dropped to his knees and bowed his head, clasping his hands in front of him. He kept his head down and stared at the floor, not saying another word. Other workers quickly joined him and kneeled before Nero.

Left standing was Tacticus.

"Hmm! What do you think, Tacticus?" asked Nero, looking over at the centurion who had been trying to stay in the background.

Tacticus took a few steps forward and looked at the altar, as if studying it. "Well, it's very … uh … big."

"Just imagine it," gushed Nero enthusiastically. "The altar lit, incense burning, and all of you bowing before me. Me, Nero, your god."

"Oh, yes, Caesar, wonderful Caesar, divine Caesar. I can just see it," sniveled Snivilus, looking up at Nero but still remaining on his knees. "I could worship you all day!"

"But Snivilus," said Nero with a sneer, "does this mean you don't worship me all day already?"

"Well … uh … um … well of course I do, Caesar. Only now you will be able to see me doing it, your worshipful. Like now."

Nero raised an eyebrow.

Tacticus swallowed hard, but said nothing. He did not kneel before Nero.

"Get up, Snivilus," Nero said. "All of you. Get up. Now. You can't place the statue of me when you're down there."

Tacticus breathed a sigh of relief.

Chapter 4

Empress Poppaea

Down in the imperial kitchens, Anna and Miriam had begun unloading the freshly baked rolls from the bakery.

"Mmm!" said Miriam. "These do smell good."

"Yes," replied Anna. "Ben bakes the best pastries in the whole Roman Empire. Nero knew what he was doing when he appointed Ben as the imperial baker."

Just then, a mean-looking woman entered the kitchen.

"Speed it up, you two! I don't have all night!" the woman shouted.

Anna jumped in fright.

"Yes, Empress Poppaea," Miriam said quickly, keeping her eyes down.

Anna gulped. The mean-looking woman was Nero's wife, Poppaea. She not only looked mean, she was mean. Everyone knew it. And now she was growing impatient, which made her even meaner.

"Give me a sample," the empress demanded. "If those

pastries are no good, they will go straight in the sewer, and the baker will go to the lions." Without waiting for Miriam, Empress Poppaea snatched up a pastry and took a bite.

Anna looked on fearfully, but she needn't have worried. The pastry melted in Poppaea's mouth.

"Mmm!" she purred. "This is divine. Utterly, utterly divine." She even began to smile, just a little.

Anna smiled back, but then she noticed a dollop of Ben's special filling oozing slowly out of the pastry. A glob fell, landing right on Empress Poppaea's sandaled foot.

"Aargh!" screamed the empress, looking down at her foot. "Why didn't you warn me about the filling?"

Anna cowered behind Miriam, too frightened to even look.

"You! Don't just stand there! Fetch me another pair of sandals!"

"Quickly," Miriam said to Anna, taking the girl by the hand and hurrying out of the kitchen. "Follow me."

Miriam led Anna into a huge room, all draped with yards and yards of fabric. Soft furs were everywhere—on the floor, on the couch, even on the bed.

"Wow!" exclaimed Anna. "Look at all the silks and fur! It must be great to live here!" She reached over to touch a white fur robe on the bed.

Miriam looked at Anna. A little frown creased her forehead. She opened her mouth as if to say something, then pinched her lips shut and turned away from the girl.

"Well, except for Nero," said Anna as she wandered around the room, running a hand down a satin drape. "And Empress Poppaea, of course. She's not nice. She's mean. And Nihilus and the guards. They're not nice either."

Then Anna noticed a beautiful vase. "Miriam, what's this?"

"That is a spice jar," said Miriam. "Poppaea thinks the spices make her smell nicer."

Anna opened the lid and sniffed the orange powder inside. "Phew!" she said. "Nicer than what? A dead goat? It … ah … ah … choo!" Anna sneezed right into the jar, and the orange powder puffed up, turning her face orange. Some of the powder landed in the flame of a nearby oil lamp and flared brightly, turning the smoke orange.

Both Anna and Miriam giggled, then Miriam quickly wiped the powder off Anna's face and off a nearby table with her apron.

"Come on," said Miriam. "We'd better get a move on and get the empress another pair of sandals. As you have already seen, the Empress Poppaea does not like to be kept waiting."

They walked into a closet as large as a small warehouse. Inside was Poppaea's wardrobe. Anna ran her hand along row after row of shiny silk gowns—deep purples, reds, gold, white, and many shades of green, from very light to very dark. She had never seen so many clothes—so many beautiful clothes.

"Miriam, is it really so bad here?" Anna asked, gazing in wonder at all the clothes she saw in the room.

"Oh, yes, child. Don't let all this richness fool you."

"Then if things are so bad here, why don't you run away?"

"I would, but I can't. It's not that easy. Nero does not take kindly to runaway servants. He can be very cruel if you are caught. And most are caught. You are supposed to think it is an honor to work in the palace. And it would be if he were a better Caesar."

"Why is he so cruel?" asked Anna.

"Oh, I don't know. Perhaps he thinks that is what being Caesar is all about."

"Is he mad? Crazy?" Anna asked, but Miriam didn't answer. There were certain questions that no one would answer out loud. Ever.

Then Anna nudged Miriam impishly. "Maybe some handsome man will come to your rescue. Perhaps a centurion. Someone like Tacticus, maybe?"

Miriam grinned and played along. "Oh, yes, I can see it now. He'll ride up in a great golden chariot and carry me off into the sunset."

"And you will go to some faraway land," Anna continued in a dreamy voice, as if she could see a vision, "and build a house in the country, and … and I could come with you." The last part she said in her own voice, a little-girl voice.

Miriam smiled at the child. "I would like that very much, Anna, especially the last part. But I am sure you will find your real parents one day."

Anna thought of the great fire then. She could still see the flames. She had been so frightened. Then she remembered the shouts as the evil Roman guards had taken her parents away. She remembered how quiet it had been after they left. She had stayed hidden for hours, afraid that the soldiers would come back and take her away too.

"That's what Ben always says, that I'll find them. But deep down I just know I'm never going to see them again." Her eyes filled with tears.

"Don't worry," Miriam said softly, gathering Anna into a gentle hug. "God is watching over you—and your parents too."

Anna nodded as she wiped the tears from her eyes.

Suddenly, they heard a loud bang. Miriam and Anna looked at each other, startled at the sound.

"What's that?" Anna cried.

Chapter 5

Worship Me!

"Be careful, you oafs!" a deep voice roared.

"It's Nero," whispered Miriam. "Shhh."

"Where is he?" Anna whispered.

"Shush! Don't worry. He can't see us. Come, let's see what's going on."

Miriam pushed aside a few of Poppaea's gowns that were right next to the wall, then pointed to a hidden grate. "Poppaea uses this to spy on Nero."

Anna giggled, covering her mouth so she wouldn't make a sound.

"Shh!" warned Miriam again as they both kneeled down to look through the grate in the wall.

They could see Nero. He was watching workers lower a huge bust of himself onto an altar.

"Easy! Take it easy! If that slips, it's the lions for all of you!"

Anna shuddered. She knew that Nero liked to feed

people to the lions during the Imperial Games. She even wondered sometimes if that was what had happened to her parents. It was possible, Ben had said once, but then quickly told her it was unlikely. She wanted to believe him, but every now and then, she didn't.

"Perfect!" shouted Nero at last. "Simply perfect!" He turned to face the men. No one moved. "Well? What are you waiting for? Worship me!"

"Oh, thank you, Caesar," spoke up a thin, weaselly soldier. "It's an honor to worship so godly a god as you, my good god."

"Yuck! Who's that?" whispered Anna.

"Snivilus," answered Miriam. "He's Nero's chief groveler."

"Oh, shut up, Snivilus," Nero said. "Just light the imperial flame."

Snivilus walked over to light the burner on the altar. But because this was the first time it had been lit, it flared up in his face before settling down.

"Cough! Cough! Hail, Caesar," wheezed Snivilus, as he threw incense into the flame.

"Yes! Hail, Nero! Lord of all!" a guard shouted.

"That's Nihilus," whispered Miriam. "He's Nero's most evil guard."

"Hail, Nero! Hail, Nero!" the other men shouted in unison as they kneeled before the altar.

Nero looked down at all the men who were kneeling and smiled. "Good. Good. This is as it should be," he said looking out over the group. Suddenly Nero saw that one soldier was not kneeling. He was standing off to one side, almost in the shadows.

"Tacticus!"

"Yes, Nero," said the centurion, who had moved away from the altar, backing toward the rear of the room.

"Tacticus. Come here. I detect some hesitancy. Have your knees been injured?"

Nihilus stood up and looked at Tacticus. He fingered the handle of his sword but didn't draw the sword from its sheath. He hated Tacticus and hoped his rival was about to commit a serious blunder.

"No, Caesar," said Tacticus. "My knees are fine."

"Then why aren't you kneeling on them with all the rest?"

Anna gripped Miriam's hand as they watched.

"Forgive me, Caesar, but …"

Nero looked menacingly at Tacticus. "But what?"

The room was silent as Nero walked slowly over to Tacticus, never taking his eyes off the soldier. "You are planning to worship me, aren't you, Tacticus?"

Tacticus hesitated.

"I'm waiting," said Nero, stopping just two feet away from Tacticus.

"I cannot."

Nero looked shocked. He took a step backward.

"Oh my, oh my," muttered Snivilus, still hunched over and kneeling. "Oh dear, oh dear. A centurion, of all people. Can you believe that? A centurion refusing to worship Nero. Oh dear, oh dear. There will be trouble now. I know it. I just know it. Whatever can Tacticus be thinking?"

Nihilus smiled. This was his chance. "I knew it," he bellowed as he ran forward, drawing his sword and raising it high as he shouted, "He's a Christian! Prepare to die, you traitor!"

Nihilus had been waiting for an opportunity just like this. He could get rid of Tacticus with one blow. And with Tacticus gone, Nihilus would be the top guard. Still holding his sword high, ready to attack, Nihilus stopped a few feet away from Tacticus.

"Wait!" commanded Nero. "How do you expect the man to worship me if you kill him? Hmmm?"

Nero turned back to Tacticus and said, "Nihilus says you are a Christian. Is he right?" Nero glared at Tacticus, who just stood at attention, looking straight ahead. He said nothing.

"Well, we shall see," Nero said, stroking his chin with one hand as he walked around the centurion. He stopped right in front of Tacticus and was silent, as if giving the soldier a chance to deny that he was a Christian.

"Tacticus, you have until my party tomorrow to either bow before me … or die! Take him away!" Nero shouted.

Miriam and Anna watched in dismay as Tacticus was grabbed roughly by three guards and marched out of the room.

Chapter 6

Danger!

Back at the bakery, Anna was excitedly telling how Tacticus had been arrested for refusing to worship Nero and how he had been taken to the dungeon by the soldiers.

"Unless Tacticus bows before Nero at the party tomorrow," Anna said, her voice going higher and higher, "he'll be executed!"

"Oh, no!" cried Helena. "That's terrible!"

"Why can't Tacticus just keep quiet about being a Christian?" said Cyrus.

Ben put his hand on the little juggler's shoulder. "We all know that following God's way can be dangerous. But it's still the best way. The only way. It was dangerous for Jesus, too, when he returned to Jerusalem."

"Why? What happened?" asked Zak, Ben's teenage apprentice.

"It was during the festival of Passover. Jerusalem was full of people all getting ready for the festival. Many people were excited to see Jesus.

"Before he reached the city of Jerusalem, Jesus and his disciples stopped in the village of Bethany, near the Mount of Olives. There, he said to two of his disciples, 'Go into the village. You will find a young donkey, one that no one has ever ridden before. Untie it and bring it here.' He also told them that if anyone asked them why they were taking the donkey, they should answer, 'The Master needs it.'

"So the two disciples went into the village and, sure enough, there was a donkey, just as Jesus had said. As they were untying the donkey, the owners came and asked them, 'Why are you untying the donkey?'

"'Our Master needs it,' they told the owners, just as Jesus had told them to say."

"Huh," said Zak, haughtily. "Jesus wouldn't travel on a common donkey."

"Ah, but that is where you are wrong, Zak," said a smiling Ben. "You see, many years before, one of the prophets had said that a true king would come to Jerusalem. But instead of riding a war horse, he would ride a donkey.

"As Jesus approached the city of Jerusalem that day, people cheered him and spread branches on the road in front of him, treating him like a king, a leader. The people had heard about Jesus and they were very excited. They thought God's chosen leader had arrived at last. They believed that Jesus had come to lead them in battle against the Roman army.

"'Hosanna! Hosanna!' called some.

"'Blessed is the one who comes in God's name,' called others.

"'Blessed is the kingdom of our father David,' shouted a young man.

"But not everyone was happy to see Jesus. Some of the religious leaders were worried by the crowd's excitement. There had been many so-called messiahs before. But this one, this Jesus, was different. Some of the leaders were afraid of him.

"These religious leaders didn't like what Jesus was telling the people, what he was teaching them. They wanted Jesus to stop teaching. They were afraid that the people would believe Jesus and stop believing what their own leaders said.

"That's why these leaders decided that Jesus had to be stopped. Jesus knew, before he went to Jerusalem, that these enemies would be waiting. But he wasn't afraid. You see, even though it was very dangerous, Jesus knew it was time to reveal who he really was."

"But Ben!" Anna blurted out, "if Tacticus does that, if he tells them that he's a Christian, Nero will kill him!"

"Not if we snatch Tacticus out of the palace first," Ben said with a smile.

"Only my best friends know I am a Christian," said Tacticus

Jesus' friends didn't know who he really was

They saw him talking to Moses and Elijah

"You must worship me!" said Nero

Miriam and Anna were in the Empress's bedroom

"Why can't Tacticus keep it a secret?"

Jesus asked his friends to fetch a donkey

People waved palm branches

"How can we rescue Tacticus from the palace?"

What excuse could they give the guards?

Miriam gave them a pile of plates to carry

Nihilus dragged Tacticus before Nero

"My gift is a story," said Tacticus

The story was about wicked workers in a vineyard

"I am your god. Worship me!" roared Nero

Tacticus and Miriam escaped

"Oh, Ben!" said Anna, as she hugged the baker.

"And I've got just the plan," said Zak, as he jumped to his feet. "Ben and I can sneak into the palace through the aqueduct."

"Zak," said Anna suspiciously, "I thought you didn't like Tacticus."

"I never said that," replied Zak. "I said I didn't trust centurions. Any centurion. Now that it looks as though he is about to lose his rank, I feel I should give him the benefit of my experience." Zak squared back his shoulders and started strutting about.

Ben smiled at his young apprentice.

"Huh!" said Anna. "How could you give Tacticus the benefit of your experience?"

Zak, a little miffed at Anna, said, "Well, he's the one in jail, not me."

"Miriam could help," Anna suggested. "She knows the palace, inside and out."

"We don't need Miriam!" said Zak cockily, sticking out his chest proudly. "Ben and I will have Tacticus out of that dungeon before the cock crows. Trust me."

"Hmm," said Anna. She decided to visit Miriam in the palace—just in case.

Chapter 7

Top Guard

"Cock-a-doodle-doo!"

"Cock-a-doodle doo!"

"We heard you the first time!" Zak snapped. It was just before dawn, and the rooster had crowed, but they still didn't have Tacticus out of the dungeon.

"Keep sawing, Zak," Ben said. He sighed. "I thought you said getting into Nero's Palace would be easy."

"How was I to know there would be bars over the aqueduct entry point? Doesn't Nero trust anyone?"

"Just keep sawing," Ben said. "Poor Tacticus must still be in the dungeon. And we can be sure that Nero won't be making life easy for him."

"I know," said Zak, clenching his teeth as he worked the saw back and forth against the stubborn the bars. "Ben, I never made life easy for Tacticus either ... but, well, he is a Roman centurion and ..."

"I know, Zak," said Ben. "You don't have to explain.

Just remember, we are not saving a centurion. We're saving a Christian."

Zak cut through another bar and started on the next.

***

Tacticus sat in his cell, waiting. He hadn't slept all night. He picked up a piece of stale bread and tossed it to a large brown rat lurking in a corner, eyeing him warily.

"Look at this cell," he said to the rat. "I'm ashamed to admit that I have sent men, women, and even children here and never given any of them a second thought."

The Roman centurion's helmet and breastplate were gone. So was his sword. He looked at the rat, who was devouring the hard piece of bread. "I'm not the old Tacticus," he told the rat. "Anna saw to that. She told me the story of the Samaritan, and I realized then how wrong I had been. I realized all the wrong I had done. But that's over. I have learned so much since then."

Tacticus watched the rat as if waiting for a reply.

Instead, he heard a voice from the dark corridor of the dungeon. "Poor Tacticus. I fear your taste in friends has taken a turn for the worse."

It was Nero, pacing the passageway outside Tacticus's cell. "You know, Tacticus, you were like a son to me. And now look at you. Stuck in here with the rats. And to think that I was going to make you Prefect of the Guard. The top post. Numero uno. Apart from me, of course. See, I even have the medallion here."

Nero stood in front of Tacticus's cell and swung the medallion from side to side in front of the bars. "Feast your eyes on it, Tacticus. Is its power not attractive to you? Just think of the opportunity."

Tacticus said nothing.

Nero sighed. "You could have been the most powerful man in Rome." Nero coughed. "Seeing as how I am a god, after all. Still, I suppose I'll just have to give the job to …" Nero paused and sighed again, "… to Nihilus."

Tacticus looked stunned. "Nihilus is an animal! You can't give him that kind of power! He will—"

"But I'm not giving it to him," said Nero nonchalantly. "You are!"

Tacticus stood up and walked over to the bars. He looked directly at Nero.

"Bow before me, Tacticus. Bow and the power shall be yours. As for Nihilus, well …" Nero shrugged his shoulders and turned to leave. "Nihilus could be useful elsewhere. One of our frontier garrisons could use another man."

Nero watched Tacticus carefully. "What do you say, Tacticus? Haven't made up your mind yet? Well, I'll leave the medallion hanging over here so you can see it.

Perhaps it will inspire you. Perhaps it will help you to reconsider. I know you will do the right thing. Prefect Tacticus. How does that sound?"

But Nero didn't wait for an answer from Tacticus. He walked out of the dungeon.

Tacticus slumped to the floor. He wasn't afraid of Nero, but he was afraid that Nihilus would get too much power. Then no Christian would be safe. And many more people would die.

"Do the right thing …" Tacticus said softly. "If only I knew what that was … "

He looked up and saw the rat, sitting again in the corner, staring at him.

***

"At last," said Zak, cutting through the final section of the gate that blocked the entry to the aqueduct. He pulled the pieces to one side. They were late. Very late. The cock had crowed long ago. It was daylight. But they might still make it to Tacticus in time if they hurried and were lucky.

"Here, Ben. Here's your guard uniform." Zak handed one uniform to Ben and started putting on the other one.

"Uh, Zak," said Ben, "my uniform appears to be a little large, even for me."

"Well, it did belong to Stouticus. We borrowed these

from the laundry. I thought you would need an extra large. Sorry."

"Humph!" said Ben, offended by Zak's view of his size. "Large would have been big enough. I am not as fat as Stouticus. See?" Ben pulled the extra cloth of the tunic out to each side and stood there, waiting for Zak to notice.

Zak smiled at the portly baker. "Come on, Ben. You'll do."

Chapter 8

Kneel or Die!

While Ben and Zak were hurrying through the palace corridors, trying to find Tacticus in the dungeon, Helena and the younger children were back in the palace kitchen unloading more trays of goodies for Nero's birthday party.

"We'll arrange the pastries on these platters," said Miriam, as she took several large plates out of a cabinet.

"Oh, Helena," said Anna, admiringly, "the decorations are beautiful!"

"Thank you, Anna," said Helena. "My Greek grandmother taught me how to do that. But dear me, it seems such a long time ago."

As the last of the pastries were placed on the platters, Miriam stood back to check their work. "Well done, everyone. Good work. Poppaea's going to think these are—"

"Awful!" shouted the Empress Poppaea, sweeping into the kitchen, her gown swirling around her.

Anna and the others stepped back, startled. "What does she mean?" whispered Anna.

"I mean," said Poppaea as she glowered at the girl, "I mean they are awful! Simply awful! Those bronze platters will not do at all!"

The Empress turned toward Miriam, who curtsied and said, "Yes, Empress," without looking up at Poppaea.

"Fetch the golden platters at once!"

"Yes, Empress," mumbled Miriam. She was relieved to learn that the only problem was the bronze platters.

While Helena and the children waited, Miriam and Anna rushed out of the kitchen and raced down a long corridor to a special storeroom. Inside, they found gleaming golden platters, lined up on shelves. Anna started to take one of the platters off a shelf, but couldn't move it. She had to use both hands. Even then it was a struggle to lift one gold platter.

"Phew!" said Anna. "Gold is heavier than I imagined. Are these plates real gold?"

"Oh, yes," replied Miriam, "real gold all the way through. That is why they are so heavy! And it was Christian slaves who were forced to dig the gold out of the mines. They did all the back-breaking work, and the emperor got all the treasure."

"Hmm," Anna said thoughtfully. She didn't like hearing stories about the hardships of Christians.

"Perhaps my parents are slaves in a gold mine now."

"Perhaps," said Miriam. "But try not to think about it."

As Anna and Miriam struggled along the passageway on their way back to the kitchen, a guard suddenly shouted, "Hey! What are you two doing here?"

Terrified, Miriam and Anna stopped, even though they were doing nothing wrong. They waited and listened, but soon realized the guard hadn't been talking to them.

"You two," shouted the guard. "Where are your papers?"

That's when they ducked into a corner so they could find out what was going on without being seen.

"Papers!" shouted the guard again. "Let me see them."

"Oh, oh," whispered Anna as she peeked out from the corner. "It's Ben and Zak. What are they doing here?"

Ben patted his soldier's disguise. "Uh … um … well, now let me see …"

"Come on, I'm waiting," said the guard.

Realizing Ben and Zak had no papers and were now in danger, Miriam, with Anna right behind her, rushed out into the hall, carrying the gold platters.

"There you are!" shouted Miriam. "We've been looking everywhere for you two." Miriam thrust her platters at Zak and Ben and, pretending to be angry, shouted, "The Empress is waiting for these and she is furious! Come at once!"

"Just a moment!" shouted the guard as other guards joined him. "Where are their papers? I must see their authorization papers. Now!"

"Commander," said Miriam, smiling at the guard, "do you know what happened the last time a guard kept the Empress waiting?"

Another guard leaned over and whispered something in the first guard's ear. His eyes opened wide with terror.

"She did? You're sure?" he asked.

The other guard nodded.

"Let them go!" the first guard ordered. "We cannot keep the Empress waiting." Then, as if to assert his power, he added, "And don't let me catch you shirking your duty again. Do you hear me?"

"Oh, yes, commander," said Ben, standing at attention. "Loud and clear."

As the guards walked off, Ben turned to Miriam and whispered, "Well done, you two. I thought we were going to be thrown into the dungeon with Tacticus."

"Now all we have to do is find Tacticus," said Zak.

"You mean you haven't found him yet?" asked Anna.

"Not yet," Zak admitted. "But now that we're inside, he's as good as free. Trust me."

Just then, there was a loud commotion at the far end of the corridor. They all ducked behind an arch. In a few minutes they saw several guards and Nihilus yanking on a chain that was looped around Tacticus, who was trying not to fall as he hurried along the corridor.

"Oh, no!" whispered Anna and Miriam together.

"At least we know where he is," said Zak.

Nihilus's cruel laugh echoed through the corridors. He stopped not far from where Ben, Zak, Anna, and Miriam were hiding. "At Nero's birthday party tonight, you will have to kneel before Nero, or die, like all the other Christians."

Nihilus was swinging the medallion Nero had hung as bait outside Tacticus's cell. He looked straight at Tacticus and, with a sneer in his voice, said, "Personally, I hope you will choose to die." Then he laughed again and continued down the corridor, swinging the medallion.

As Tacticus was dragged away, Nihilus's vile laughter could be heard echoing in the passageways.

"Kneel or die, Tacticus," Nihilus shouted. "Kneel or die."

Chapter 9

Poppaea's New Gowns

The Empress Poppaea was pacing back and forth in her dressing rooms at the Imperial Palace.

"Where are they? They should have been here by now," she said to no one in particular.

The empress, months ago, had ordered one hundred new gowns to be made of the finest silks and the softest cotton. She hadn't trusted the palace seamstresses with the job. Instead, she had found a shop in Rome known for its original designs, its careful stitching, the dyes it used. The shop owner had promised that ten gowns would be ready long before Nero's birthday.

Poppaea was in a rage. "If they don't get here, I'll have nothing to wear," she wailed.

Her attendants tried to stay out of her way, scurrying first one way, then the other, as the empress paced.

Poppaea had already had her bath. Her hair had been arranged carefully. Her jewels were ready to be put on.

Even her perfumes and spices had been carefully sprayed and puffed to offer just the right fragrance.

She was standing in the middle of one of the rooms, carefully checking her makeup in a mirror, when there was a soft knock at the door. A servant immediately went to the door and opened it.

In walked a parade of servants, each carrying one of the long, flowing gowns made specially for the empress. The fabric of some was so sheer you could almost see through it, and they shimmered in the light.

On seeing the gowns, the Empress Poppaea forgot her anger. She rushed toward the first servant and ran her hands over the shimmering silk draped across the young woman's arms. She then went to the next, and the next, so excited she could do nothing but smile and say "ooh" and "aah." Then Poppaea had the servants stand in a large semicircle so she could see all of the gowns and compare them and—finally—choose one for Nero's birthday.

Chapter 10

Happy Birthday, Nero

"Hush, everyone," whispered Miriam. "This is Empress Poppaea's bedroom. If we're caught here …"

"Yes, quite," whispered Ben. "Now where is this grate which allows us to spy on Nero?"

"Over here, in Poppaea's closet," replied Miriam as she led Ben, Helena, and the children across the room.

"Wow!" said little Marcus. "Look at all these gowns! How can one person need so many?"

"Never mind that," said Justin. "Just look through here. We have to see what's going on."

Marcus peered through the grate in the wall as the sound of drums and trumpets blared. "Look at that huge altar! It's got a statue of Nero in the middle! Come, look. Quick!"

"And there's Tacticus," said Justin. "Ben, he's being watched by Nihilus. How are we going to get to him?"

"We'd have to be royalty to get down there," said Zak disgustedly.

Anna and Miriam looked around at the Empress Poppaea's extravagant gowns. Then they turned to each other and smiled knowingly.

***

Later that evening, down in Nero's Great Hall, Nero was strumming his lyre and singing a birthday song to himself:

> *"Happy birthday to me*
> *As a god I decree*
> *For now and forever*
> *You shall all worship me."*

"Wonderful, Nero, simply wonderful. Isn't he wonderful to write such a song, everyone? So talented, so tuneful, so …" Snivilus continued to grovel before Nero, staying close enough so Nero could hear every word.

Suddenly there was a commotion at the back of the hall as Ben and the gang entered. Swathed in the Empress Poppaea's elaborate gowns, veils covering their faces, they made a spectacular sight.

"I am the Princess Benwina," said Ben in a high, haughty voice, "and these are my sisters. We have come to pay homage to Caesar on this joyous occasion."

"I'm so embarrassed," whispered Zak to Anna. "This will never work."

"Yes, it will," she said as she adjusted Zak's veil. "And you look lovely."

Zak scowled at her.

The Empress Poppaea sat a bit straighter and peered at the newcomers. There was something familiar about them. But she couldn't see very well at that distance. She decided to take another look when they got closer.

Nero, as was his way, had ignored the interruption because he hadn't finished singing his song. "Shall all worship me …" he crooned.

Clapping his hands, Snivilus gushed, "Oh, you know we will, Caesar. How could we not worship you? Right, everybody?"

As Nero's courtiers applauded, Snivilus turned and, clapping his hands, shouted, "Bring forth Caesar's gifts, and let the worshiping commence!"

A huge slave banged a gong. The courtiers, bearing gifts, formed a line before Nero. A troop of acrobats rushed to the front of the line, all bowing down as one before the Emperor.

"Our gift to Caesar is the gift of amusement!" they said in unison and, with a series of back flips, tumbles, and somersaults, performed before Nero.

"Huh!" said an unimpressed Cyrus, as he peeked

through Empress Poppaea's spy grate. "It's all been done. My father could have done those tricks in his sleep with one hand tied behind his back. Those guys are amateurs."

In a final flourish, the acrobats did somersaults until they were right in front of the altar. Then they threw some incense into the flame on the top of Nero's altar and shouted, "Hail, Nero! Lord of all!"

"Not bad," purred Nero, studying the acrobats. "Not bad at all."

"Not bad, my eye," Cyrus muttered. "Why, my father could do a triple back flip before breakfast. This lot couldn't flip a coin."

Next in line was Antonius, a sharp-featured little man with eyes like a weasel. "My gift to Caesar is the gift of string." He held up a ball that looked like nothing more than string because that's all it was—string.

"String!" snarled Caesar, and signaled the guards to take Antonius away.

"And this gold amulet," Antonius added quickly, pulling a gold charm from a leather thong around his neck.

"Hmm," muttered Nero. He allowed Antonius to throw some incense into the fire on the altar before leaving.

"Oh, no," whispered Marcus from his hiding place in the Empress Poppaea's closet. "Nihilus and Tacticus are next."

"Your turn, traitor," snarled Nihilus as he jerked a chain attached to Tacticus's wrists.

Nero was now very interested in what would happen next. He leaned forward. "Ah! Tacticus! And what shall your gift be? Hmm? Your worship or your life?"

A hush fell over the court as Nihilus fingered his sword in anticipation.

"My gift to Caesar," said Tacticus softly, "is a story."

"Excellent!" shouted Nero excitedly, clapping his hands. "I always enjoy a good tale. Begin, begin. I'm comfortable."

Tacticus looked up at Nero, then at the others nearby. He began to speak, slowly and softly. "This story was told by a very great man. It is about someone who planted a new vineyard."

"A vineyard," interrupted Nero. "Good. A good beginning. Which reminds me, Snivilus. Do fetch me a glass of wine. I enjoy a glass of wine with a good story."

While Snivilus shuffled off, Tacticus said, "The man rented the vineyard out to some farmers. The farmers had a good year. After the harvest, the owner of the vineyard sent one of his servants to collect his share of the profits. But the servant was beaten badly and had to return to his master empty-handed.

"The owner of the vineyard sent another servant. But the farmers beat him too. The owner sent more servants and there was even more violence. Finally, some servants were killed.

"The owner of the vineyard did not know what to do. He turned to his son and said, 'Perhaps if I send you, my son, they will show more respect.'

"The son nodded in agreement and very soon, he was on his way to see the farmers. It did not take the farmers long to realize who he was.

"'It is the owner's son,' said one farmer.

"'The vineyard will belong to him when his father dies,' said another.

"'Not necessarily,' said the first farmer as he picked up a heavy wooden club.

"The owner of the vineyard was soon told the bad news. The farmers had killed his only son. The owner screamed out in anguish at the news."

Tacticus paused.

"How wonderful," said Nero. "The treachery! The deceit! Wonderful! Isn't it wonderful, everyone?"

There were a few cheers.

"Truly. Truly it is wonderful," Snivilus said as he returned with a carafe of wine for Nero.

Nero rubbed his hands together gleefully. He could hardly wait for the rest of the story.

Snivilus continued his praise. "Wonderful story, Tacticus. What deceit. Nero loves it. What a mind to conjure up such a story."

"Yes," agreed Nero. "The man who first told this story must have been great indeed."

"Oh, yes, he was," Tacticus agreed. "In fact, he was speaking to the leaders of his religion at the time."

"The leaders!" gushed Nero. "You don't say. Do tell me more. There must be more, surely. Go on, Tacticus."

Tacticus cleared his throat and said, "Well, the person who first told the story to the religious leaders went on to ask a question. He asked them, 'And what will the vineyard owner do, now that his son has been killed?'"

"He'll go to the vineyard and kill the tenants," replied Nero gleefully, not waiting for a reply from anyone else. "That's what I would do. Yes, that's exactly what I would do. Kill the tenants who killed my son."

"That is just what he did," said Tacticus, smiling at Nero. "And he gave the vineyard to new tenants."

"Excellent, Tacticus. What a good story. I like a good story. But tell me, the 'great man' who first told the story …" Nero got up from his throne and walked straight up to Tacticus. He stood there, just a couple feet away, and looked the centurion straight in the eye. "What was his name?"

"Jesus," came Tacticus's confident reply. "It was Jesus, the Christ. My Lord."

The courtiers gasped. Even Snivilus was shocked as

Nero pushed his face right up to Tacticus and whispered menacingly, "Your Lord? How dare you! I am your god! You shall bow down and worship me! Now!"

Tacticus stood his ground and even though his reply to Nero was as soft as a whisper, everyone heard him. "I would rather die!"

"And so you shall!" roared Nero. "So you shall!"

Nero turned from Tacticus and looked out at the people gathered in the hall. "All of you! Hear me! I shall kill all Christians if it is the last thing I do!"

Nero quickly turned around and screamed, "Nihilus! Slay this insolent dog at once!"

"With pleasure, Caesar," said the evil guard.

Nihilus raised his sword and took a step toward Tacticus.

Chapter 11

Orange Smoke

Her face tight with fear and concentration, Miriam watched as Nihilus approached Tacticus. Timing was everything . . .

"Now!" Miriam said to Anna.

Whooping triumphantly, they each tipped one of the Empress's spice vases onto Nero's altar. Poof! A huge plume of thick orange smoke instantly filled the room. Courtiers screamed and fled in every direction. Nero's celebration turned into utter confusion. People crashed into each other as they tried to get away from the choking, orange smoke. No one knew what had happened. No one could see.

Blindly, Nihilus swung his sword in Tacticus's direction, but the centurion ducked away, and the sword embedded itself in Nero's altar. Tacticus shoved Nihilus aside and bolted.

"Snivilus!" shouted Nero angrily, his arms waving, trying desperately to clear the air. "Tacticus … he's getting away! Get after him!"

Snivilus tried to feel his way toward the spot where Tacticus had been standing, but he was too late. Tacticus had escaped.

Meanwhile, Ben and the gang ripped off their gowns and wrapped two of them over the guards' heads. Shouting and swearing, the blinded men ripped and tugged at the gowns, trying to free themselves.

"Quick," said Ben to Zak, "tie these gowns together to make a rope."

As the Imperial Guards moved toward Tacticus, Ben pulled the rope of gowns across a doorway, and the guards tripped on the rope and fell, sprawling in a tangle.

Marcus, who had caught the action from his spot behind the grate, said, "Look, Ben and Zak have tripped the guards!"

Cyrus and Justin pushed closer to the grating to get a better look, then fell back in fits of laughter. The guards, scrambling to get back in the chase, had knocked the Empress Poppaea into a fountain. She came up spluttering and screaming, drenched from head to foot.

"That is the funniest thing I have ever seen," said Cyrus, laughing.

Marcus and Justin giggled with delight.

Below, in the Great Hall, the guards were still tangled in Poppaea's silks and looked something like a troupe of dancers. But one by one they freed themselves and soon were making their way through the smoke toward Tacticus's rescuers—Helena, Ben, Zak, Anna, and Miriam. They had to get away, but how?

"We've got you now," said one particularly large soldier, as he looked down at Zak. It was Stouticus, the worst soldier in the entire Roman army. He was holding his sword in one hand, a pastry in the other.

"Guess again!" shouted Justin as he dropped a rope down to the gang. He and Cyrus and Marcus had made the rope out of some of Empress Poppaea's gowns, then tied one end to the massive bed in Poppaea's bedroom.

"Get them!" screamed Nero from his throne, wiping orange powder from his eyes. "After them!"

As Ben and Zak and the rest of the gang climbed up the wall leading to the spy grate, using the silk rope, Cyrus shouted, "Time for plan two, Marcus!"

Marcus tossed a basket of Ben's famous pastries down through the hole. They landed right in front of Stouticus.

"Ahh! Mmm! That smell," said Stouticus as he looked down at the basket of pastries. "Seems a shame to let them go to waste. After all, they would only get trampled on." He bent down to pick up the basket.

Just then one of the running guards slammed into the back of the bent-over centurion. "Stouticus, you idiot!" he shouted just before his head hit the floor. One after another, the guards went sprawling, tangled in the mound of bodies that had Stouticus at the base.

"Look!" yelled a soldier who was able to stop in time. "They're escaping! Right through that hole in the wall. Grab that rope!"

But just as he said that, Ben, the last to climb the wall using the silk rope, squeezed through the hole and pulled the rope up behind him. Ben and the others vanished.

"Quick," said a guard, "if we climb up and over Nero's altar, we might be able to climb up there and catch them."

"We'd better catch them," said another, "or we'll be a lion's breakfast."

Stouticus gulped. He loved eating but he did not want to be there when the lions were eating. "I'll go first," he said. "I'm the centurion."

"Oh, no!" yelled the others.

Stouticus began climbing up Nero's new altar toward the hole that led to Empress Poppaea's bedroom.

By this time, the orange smoke had cleared and Nero could see what was going on. "What … who … oh no!" he said as the altar began to teeter under the weight of the fat centurion. "Who sent that big buffoon up there? That's my altar! My statue!"

Nero stood up and wildly waved his arms as he ran toward the altar. "Get down, you clodhead! It's going to fall. Get down you clumsy … get down … aargh!"

Just then, the huge bust of Nero began to teeter, then

crashed onto its side, breaking into pieces and smashing Nero's altar and his throne.

"Nero," wailed the Empress Poppaea, dragging long strips of her new gowns. "Look! Look!"

"I'm looking!" screamed Nero.

"Nero!" Empress Poppaea screamed again. "Look at my gowns! Look at what those fools have done to my beautiful gowns!"

"Gowns!" Nero yelled. "Never mind your ugly gowns! Look at my altar! Look at what those clodheads have done to my beautiful altar!"

Just then, from a balcony overlooking the Great Hall, the gang shouted, "Happy birthday, Caesar!"

"Nihilus!" screamed Nero. "Catch those treacherous cretins and—" Nero stopped screaming and looked around. Nihilus was nowhere to be seen.

Nero sat down on a step leading to his mangled throne, forlorn and wailing. "Nihilus? Nihilus? No. Not you too. You haven't abandoned me too, have you? Nihilus? Nihilus!"

Chapter 12

Old Enemies

The corridors of the palace echoed with the shouts of guards and the thunder of running feet as Miriam led the gang through some of the lesser known areas of the Imperial Palace. "This old service tunnel should lead us right to your wagon at the back of the kitchen," she said, pointing.

"We can't thank you enough," said Ben, huffing and puffing as he ran.

"Oh, I had my reasons for helping," said Miriam, as she flashed a smile at Tacticus.

Anna thought she actually saw Tacticus blush.

"I can't believe we got away from those guards," said Cyrus. Suddenly he stopped in his tracks. "Well, almost!"

A large silhouette appeared in front of them, almost at the end of the tunnel.

"Nihilus!" said Tacticus.

"He's blocking the exit," said Ben. "There's no escape."

"Stay close, everyone," cautioned Helena. "There is no telling what that evil man will do."

"Let me through," said Tacticus as he pushed to the front of the small group.

"It's me you want, Nihilus!" Tacticus shouted. "Let the others go!"

Nihilus shook his head and continued to walk toward them, knowing he had them all trapped. "All enemies of the Empire must be executed … including the little ones. That is Nero's order. You know that, Tacticus. You used to be one of us, remember?"

Nihilus drew his sword as he continued walking toward the group.

Tacticus knew that, like the owner of the vineyard in Jesus' story, he would have to take action against this evil. But what could he do? There was no time to think. He just had to act.

Nihilus lunged at Tacticus with his sword.

The two warriors' swords clanked loudly as they hit, then scraped against each other.

"I pity you, Tacticus," hissed Nihilus, circling for another try. "You had everything and you threw it all away. Your Christian friends have blinded you."

"You're the one who is blind, Nihilus!"

Nihilus lunged again at Tacticus, but Tacticus dodged to one side, using his sword handle to knock Nihilus's sword away.

When Nihilus stumbled, falling to one knee, Tacticus shouted, "Go!"

Ben and the others needed no other instructions. They all ran toward the daylight at the tunnel entrance.

Tacticus watched as his friends raced down the tunnel toward freedom. As he neared the entrance, Cyrus stopped and turned to look back. "Tacticus! Watch out!" he shouted.

Tacticus turned just in time to see Nihilus, who had grabbed a flaming torch from the tunnel wall, fling the torch at him.

Tacticus dodged the flame, backing his way toward the entrance, but Nihilus swung his heavy sword, sending Tacticus's sword flying.

"Oh, no!" shouted Miriam as she ran back to help Tacticus.

"Oh, yes!" sniggered Nihilus. "I shall enjoy watching you die, Tacticus."

"Tacticus!" shouted Miriam, as she ran behind Nihilus, picked up Tacticus's heavy sword, and threw it to him.

Tacticus caught his sword just as Nihilus charged again. This time, Tacticus blocked Nihilus's attack. Then he sent his opponent's sword flying with a number of strong blows.

"Hurray!" shouted Justin, Marcus, and Cyrus from a safe distance.

Now it was Nihilus who was defenseless. "Well now, Christian," he taunted, "you had better kill me. Because if you don't, I'll come after you."

"I know you will," spat Tacticus, as he drew back his sword.

Justin, Marcus, and Cyrus drew in a sharp breath, and Ben stepped in front of them so they wouldn't see anything.

Nihilus, surprised that Tacticus had agreed with him, put his arms up to surrender just as Tacticus swung his sword down swiftly.

"Aargh!" screamed Nihilus, closing his eyes.

The gang stiffened, covering their eyes with their hands.

"Oh!" whispered Marcus.

Suddenly, there was a great clang.

Cyrus peeked through his fingers. "He didn't kill Nihilus! He didn't kill Nihilus!"

Tacticus had cut the chain that held up the gate near the entrance to the tunnel. Nihilus was trapped inside the tunnel, and Tacticus was outside, free.

Tacticus stuck his nose against the iron gate and hissed at his enemy, "One day I may have to kill you, Nihilus, but not today."

"Hurray! Hurray for Tacticus!" cheered the gang.

As they were walking away, they heard Nihilus shout, "I will find you, Tacticus! I will find all of you! This isn't the end! It's just the beginning!"

Chapter 13

Welcome to the Underground

Traveling down one of the back streets of Rome, Ben and the gang headed toward home.

Tacticus was sitting in the back of the bakery wagon enjoying the ride, looking up at the moon, when he began chuckling to himself.

"What's so funny?" asked Ben.

"You are, you and Zak," said Tacticus, grinning broadly. "I've never been rescued by a pack of princesses before." Then he looked very serious as he added, "And I don't know how to thank you."

"Thank Anna and Miriam," said Zak. "It was their plan."

"Thank you," Tacticus said as he turned to Anna, touching her hand.

"And thank you, Miriam," he said, looking at the young woman with open awe and admiration. "Without you, we would never have escaped from the palace. Even

I didn't know about that last tunnel."

Anna and Miriam shared a secret grin. Tacticus hadn't saved Miriam, after all. Instead, Miriam had saved Tacticus!

Ben turned a corner and steered the horse down another alley. The rhythmic clip-clop of the horse's hooves echoed between the buildings. The silvery path of the moon was straight ahead, lighting their way.

Ben turned sideways in the driver's seat and said, "You know, Tacticus, that Nihilus meant what he said. I'm afraid your old life as a centurion is over."

The big Roman soldier grinned. "I know."

Zak, who had been quiet as they rode along, slapped Tacticus heartily on the back. "Welcome to the Christian underground, centurion."

"Thank you, Zak. Thank you all." Tacticus gave a broad smile, then looked quickly at Miriam.

Their eyes met for a long moment, and Miriam smiled.